Gran, You've Got Mail!

Gran, You've Got Mail!

JO HOESTLANDT

Illustrations by Aurélie Abolivier

Translated from the French by Y. Maudet

DELACORTE PRESS

Published by Delacorte Press
an imprint of Random House Children's Books
a division of Random House, Inc.
New York

Text copyright © 1999 by Editions Nathan, Paris, France, for the first edition,
© 2006 Editions Nathan, Paris, France, for the current edition
Translation copyright © 2008 by Y. Maudet
Notes © 2008 by Delacorte Press
Illustrations copyright © 2006 by Aurélie Abolivier
Originally published in France in 1999 under the title *Mémé, t'as du Courier!*

Visit us on the Web! www.randomhouse.com/kids

Educators and librarians, for a variety of teaching tools, visit us at
www.randomhouse.com/teachers

Library of Congress Cataloging-in-Publication Data
Hoestlandt, Jo.
[Mémé t'as du Courier. English]
Gran, you've got mail! / Jo Hoestlandt ; illustrations by Aurélie Abolivier ;
translated from the French by Y. Maudet. — 1st ed.
p. cm.
Summary: Lively letters between a self-centered young girl and her wise great-
grandmother reveal generational differences and a deep affection for each other.
ISBN: 978-0-385-73565-0 (trade)
ISBN: 978-0-385-90553-4 (Gibraltar lib. bdg.) [1. Great-grandmothers—Fiction.
2. Letters—Fiction.] I. Abolivier, Aurélie, ill. II. Maudet, Y. III. Title.
IV. Title: Gran, you have got mail!
PZ7.H67145Gr 2008
[Fic]—dc22
2007045753

The text of this book is set in 12-point Bembo.

Printed in the United States of America

10 9 8 7 6 5 4 3 2 1

First American Edition

To my gran, of course
—J.H.

To my aunt
—A.A.

Gran, You've Got Mail!

October 17

Dear Gran,

It's been a long time since I've written to you, so you'll be surprised to get this letter. Don't worry—nothing bad has happened. I just want to practice typing on the computer that Dad bought me a few months ago. Every weekend he nags me to learn the keyboard. So here I am. But I have no intention of keeping a diary—especially an electronic one. I think it's weird, even a little nuts, to write to yourself.

Of course, I'm not sure I'll have much to tell you, but we'll see.

Now that you're almost ninety years old, I don't expect you'll answer me very often. I know you no longer see very well. But I'd rather that my chore of

1

learning the keyboard please someone, and I've decided it will be you. So I'll type, print, and mail my letters off.

I'm stopping now; I've practiced enough for today. More another time.

Annabelle

P.S. Sorry for the typos if there are any. I'm just a beginner and don't have time to spellcheck.

October 29

Dear Gran,

It's me again. I'm bugged because you haven't answered my first letter. I wish you'd make an effort. Mom always says you'd like to hear from your great-grandchildren now and then, but I wonder if she made that up. Maybe you couldn't care less. Maybe it's even a big pain for you to go to the mailbox to pick up your mail. After all, when I saw you last Christmas, your foot was swollen and I thought that with a ribbon tied around it, it would look a lot like a wrapped present. Of course, I'm sure having a foot in your condition is no gift.

Well, I hope I haven't offended you.

Now for some news.

First, the weather is rotten. Second, the weather

is rotten. And finally, the weather is still rotten. I can't hang around in town with my friends without getting drenched, which is really annoying.

I'll sign off now. I want to watch a show on TV that I never miss.

And you, is there a TV show that you really like?

Kisses,
Annabelle

November 2

My dear Annabelle,

I received your two letters.

If I didn't answer the first one right away, it's because I didn't realize you were in such a hurry. Sorry.

First, blessed be your computer, since it gives me the chance to hear from you! It's indeed the first time I find an advantage to this modern contraption that seemed so barbaric to me until now.

Of course, I remember the handwritten letters you sent me when you were six or seven years old, with all their charming spelling mistakes. I still have them, actually. They're precious to me. Especially since you haven't sent me many others since then. In one of them, you thanked me for the little doll that I offered you and that you named Simone—after me—to please me. I even remember that as she grew older, this doll became rather ugly, and that you took a certain delight in saying:

"The older she gets, the more my doll looks like you, Gran."

It was probably true, even if this didn't please me much.

But all this was before you requested nothing more than a check for Christmas.

I'll take advantage of this letter to tell you that if, given my age, it suits me not to go shopping to buy you and your two brothers something you might like, it upsets me to send you a check—as if I'm paying the gas bill or my income taxes.

It bothers me even more that you never write to tell me what you bought with my checks. Sometimes I wonder if you simply make confetti out of them. . . .

You tell me you're having rotten weather. It rains often here too, but the trees are displaying magnificent colors and I stay at my window as much as I can to enjoy the show.

That's all for today, because it won't be long before my neighbor arrives. She comes every afternoon around five o'clock to play Scrabble with me. It helps us kill time, as well as keep the neurons of our brains in shape. I prefer that to any TV program.

Big hug,
Gran

November 7

Dear Gran,

Thank you for your first letter. It gave me so much pleasure. I still keep my doll Simone at the foot of my bed, although, of course, I haven't played with her in a long time. (I don't know if you remember, but I'm twelve now.)

Today the sun is shining and the sky is blue. It's Friday, and as soon as I finish practicing on the computer, I'm meeting up with some friends. We're going to a movie theater to see *Titanic*—an awesomely tragic movie that I've already seen twice.

So goodbye for now.

Until next time . . .

Big hug,
Annabelle

November 10

My dear Annabelle,

    What a pity to go to the movies when the weather is nice, and to see a tragic movie, no less!

    There are already enough catastrophes in life (in my opinion), so why go to a movie to see any more?

    I don't remember the sinking of the <u>Titanic</u>. I was only four years old at the time.

    There can't be many survivors still alive, and I can't imagine that it must be very pleasant for them to relive their nightmare on the big screen.

    In any case, you'd be better off playing outside when the sun is shining.

It's five o'clock and my neighbor, Mrs. Fouillich (did I mention her to you before?), is coming over to play Scrabble with me.

Kisses from your old Gran

November 20

Dear Gran,

You're wrong when it comes to *Titanic*. It's a great movie, full of emotion. Of course, it's just a movie and probably better that way. When I think that such a big ship really did sink, it makes me shudder. Not to mention that the main character is so cute, but that's not the only reason the movie is amazing. My friends and I agree that it's the best movie we've ever seen. Much better than *Gone with the Wind*, which I watched on TV and found pretty dull and slow going, if you know what I mean.

How is your foot? Does it still look giftwrapped?

As for me, I'm feeling bored.

I don't know whether I told you, but I have a

friend named Lucia. Or rather, I had a friend named Lucia. She's still called Lucia, but what I mean is that she's no longer my friend.

I hope you won't make fun of me. At home they couldn't care less that Lucia and I aren't talking to each other. They only think about themselves. Mom thinks only of telling me over and over again that I should try to do better in school. That I should be grateful that she gave up part of the kitchen (when it was renovated) so I could have my own room. As for Dad, he thinks about work, and Jules and Jonathan argue and fight as soon as they're together. Sometimes I really get fed up with this family.

I'll sign off now because I'm feeling cold. Mom keeps the windows in my room open for hours, and in this season, it's freezing.

I give you a big kiss, little Gran.

Annabelle

P.S. Don't get mad if I tell you this, but you repeat yourself. You've already told me twice that your neighbor, Mrs. Fouillis or something like that, comes to play Scrabble with you at five o'clock. I get the picture!

December 2 or 3

My dear Annabelle,

How could you say that <u>Gone with the Wind</u> is dull? It's probably because you only saw it on TV! It's a fantastic movie and Clark Gable is the most attractive man I've ever laid eyes on! If they were to show it again in a movie theater, I would try to go in spite of my bad foot. I saw the movie with my mother a long time ago. God, so long ago . . . But I can still remember my mother, her eyes as shiny with tears as mine. We both loved the picture. My dear Annabelle, at least we're in agreement on one point: When the story is good, a movie is truly magical.

You tell me that your friendship with Lucia is over.

How did this happen? Are you sure you're not mistaken? Why don't you talk it over with her? You should force yourself to approach her, my dear. It requires more humility than pride to love a friend.

I tell you this because I stupidly lost a close friend myself long ago, and your letter brought it all back. It still hurts a lot, seventy years or so later. You can't get over a lost friendship.

As for my foot, let's say that it still looks gift-wrapped, but smaller than the last time you saw me.

A big hug to my little darling.

Let's hope you don't grow tired of the computer your father gave you. Give him a kiss for me, and to the rest of the family.

Gran

P.S. Pardon me if I repeat myself at times. I'm happy to write to you and to receive your mail, but once I've sent a letter, I just can't remember what I've said. If you want mail that isn't repetitious, write to your cousin Amélie.

December 10

Dear Gran,

Writing to Cousin Amélie is not a possibility. I can't stand her. If she doesn't repeat herself, it's only because she has nothing to say! Today my letter will be short; I have to study for a history exam, and typing on the computer won't help me memorize the list of caliphs from the Umayyad dynasty. The only one I manage to remember is Abd al-Rahmān, because he escaped a terrible massacre when his family was overthrown from power in Syria.

I really wonder why we have to remember the names of the slaughtered ones. Well, that's the way it is. . . .

Until next time, my dear old Gran,

Annabelle

December 15

My dear Annabelle,

It's snowing! From my armchair by the window, I'm watching the dance of the flakes. I still marvel at this sight. I have to remember to put some buttered bread on the windowsill for the birds, the poor fellows. But to come back to your last letter, if with so few lines one can even call it that. Well, anyway . . .

I've never heard of these Umayyads, and I think they make you learn very difficult things in school. Yet there is one thing I do know, and it's that the names of the slaughtered ones, as you say, are just as important to remember as the names of the ones who do the slaughtering. Even more so, if you ask me.

Nowadays I know that the new generations don't care much about celebrating the past, November 11th in particular, when the dead from the First World War—or the slaughtered ones—are honored.

Well, you see, my dear, each year on November 11th, I remember my three brothers, who were killed in 1917, at the Chemin des Dames, and whose names are engraved on the war memorial in the village where we were born, and where they never returned to. And I'm pleased that one day a year, the slaughtered ones can be remembered. Whether it be the slaughtered Umayyads you mentioned, and for whom I feel sorry, or my brothers, who did not deserve their fate.

Well, all this is rather gloomy.

I don't have the courage to continue.

I'm sorry if I've saddened you.

Your Gran, who thinks of you

The following day

I don't know why I rehashed the past like that. I got so sidetracked that I forgot to tell you the most important news.

My cat had two lovely kittens. I gave one away but kept the other. Age must be making me sentimental. Or else, with Christmas so near, I guess I wanted to give you something special this year.

This kitten is tiger orange, and looks like the one that I begged my grandmother to keep when I was about your age. She agreed, grumpily. I'm keeping this one grumpily too. If you want it, it's yours. But don't wait too long to come and pick it up, because in a few days it will start scratching my curtains and armchair. This will annoy me and make me regret I didn't get rid of it also.

Kisses from your Gran

25

P.S. Did you make up with your friend? I forget her name.

December 19

Dear Gran,

Hooray! Vacation! Just in time too, because I was fed up with school.

The teachers go nuts at the end of each term, giving a test here and a test there. They don't act like teachers, but like grading robots!

I can't say how happy I am! I'm reading your last letter again.

My poor Gran, I didn't know that your brothers had died in the First World War. I didn't even know that you had brothers. Why is it you never told us? And why is it that Mom and Dad never mentioned it? Are you sure they know about it?

It's horrible what happened! How can you possibly lose three brothers at once?

I only have Jules and Jonathan, and I can't imagine that they could both die at the same time. I'd become an only child!

I think nothing could help soothe my grief. Not even a November 11th parade around a war memorial.

Well, now that you're old, that may be why the sound of a parade band makes you feel better. The only thing that could help me would be to hear the church organ. I went to a funeral once; you'll remember, it was for Aunt Pauline, who I didn't know very well. But when I listened to the organ at church, I started to cry as if Aunt Pauline had been a fantastic person, someone I adored. Well, it's weird. It's too bad you have to be dead to be entitled to such music, because, of course, you can take advantage of it only when other people die, not at your own funeral. Except if you can hear it from your coffin or from heaven. But that would be surprising, don't you think?

Mom just came in to see what I'm up to. I told her I was writing to you on the computer. She thought that was a good idea. Then when she noticed I was talking about Aunt Pauline and funerals, she made a face and suggested I come up with a different topic, considering your age and all.

I don't mind doing that, but what else should I write about?

After all, you're the one who brought up your brothers dying during the 1914–1918 war.

I've been thinking again about my two brothers and the fact that they never stop killing enemies on their video games. I wouldn't like to see either of them killed in a war, but a little wound, nothing too serious, might teach them a lesson. What do you think?

As for my ex-friend Lucia, no change. Ever since

we both got a zero on a math test, she stopped liking me. I won't say any more.

Kisses to you, Gran, from the great-granddaughter you adore.

Annabelle

December 24, Christmas Eve
Hooray! Hooray!

Dear Gran,

How come you didn't answer my last letter?

Is it because I wrote about funerals? If that's the case, I'm sorry; if it's for another reason, please tell me what it is.

You can't imagine how many crazy scenarios have been running through my mind.

Or is it because I didn't answer you about the kitten you're keeping for me? It's too bad you gave the other one away, because now I don't have a choice. I keep telling myself that I might have liked that one better.

You see, people always do the choosing for me—which gets on my nerves. For instance, earlier this year I was hesitating between ballet lessons and judo classes, like Jules and Jonathan take (if only to prove to them that I could do it, and maybe even show them a thing or two).

Mom registered me for ballet, saying it would help me be more graceful. Thanks a lot! Anyway, what's the use of being more graceful at school? The girls just think I'm stuck-up, and the boys stick to me like chewing gum. But with judo, they wouldn't dare!

Another example: At dinner, by the time I decide on a piece of meat, everyone has already helped themselves. I end up taking what's left.

And now you choose my cat.

In any case, Mom will never let me bring a cat home. Especially if it pees on the rugs and tears the curtains to pieces.

Mom will say that if I want a pet, I have to get one that won't vandalize the house. And by the time I decide on a pet, she'll have brought me a stupid bright yellow canary who'll sing his head off every morning. Talk about a racket!

As you can see, Gran, I'm a little upset tonight. It's Christmas Eve and I spent all my money on presents for everybody. I wonder if they deserve them.

Jules and Jonathan bug me nonstop. They keep coming into my room without knocking first. If they see their presents, too bad for them! They just won't be surprised on Christmas Day. Jules told me he didn't get me anything because he had no money left. I hope he's just teasing, because when I think of all the money I spent on him—it would be too unfair.

Gran, I'm sending you a nice drawing that I made on the computer. Dad congratulated me on it. I hope you'll like it too. Merry Christmas, dear Gran. Dad and Mom wrote to you, and I'm adding their letter to mine. I wish your foot would get better.

I kiss you with all my heart.

Your great-granddaughter, who loves you,
Annabelle

January 1

My dear great-granddaughter,

At the very beginning of this new year, I wish you good health and a lot of happiness with your family and friends.

Your parents phoned, and I understand that the year started out well! I'm talking about the beautiful gift they gave you. A camera! I hope you'll send me some of the family pictures you took on Christmas Day. I don't have that many, and it would make me happy. But what I would love even more is a photo of just my Annabelle.

I also want to thank you for your letters. Each one of them gives me immense pleasure.

I'm sure that very few great-grandmothers are as lucky as I am.

Happy new year, my darling.
I kiss you with all my loving heart.

Your Gran, who thinks of you often

January 8

Dear Gran,

Happy new year to you too. The new year isn't starting so well for me, though. I had a bad day. I got a 3 on my test about those stupid Umayyads.

What makes things worse is that I mentioned them to you, so I guess I had the feeling I knew a lot about them. But once I was staring at the questions on my sheet of paper, I couldn't think of anything but your three brothers. Bad luck, right?

At least I scored some points for knowing that Abd al-Rahmān survived the massacre. So I guess my test score could have been worse—like a big fat zero. Although I might have been better off with a zero.

At school, sometimes it's cooler to get a 0 than a 3. Three is zilch. Zero has oomph.

(I don't remember if I ever mentioned the zero I got once on a math test.) Zero in math, three in history . . .

I'm annoyed to start off the year with a rotten test score. I had made lots of good resolutions too! Guess I'm really not lucky.

Till next time, my dear Gran,
a desperate Annabelle

January 21

Anniversary of Louis XVI's death, right?
I hate to think about all those people who
got beheaded!
It's enough to make me puke (pardon the
expression).

Dear Gran,

Still no answer from you. I was beginning to
worry, so I asked Mom and Dad for your telephone
number. I called: no answer. Not even from an
answering machine. You really live in another
world, Gran!

Don't take it badly, but it's true. You don't have a
dishwasher, and you have a funny little coffee
grinder that hurts your hands and collects the grinds
in a little drawer. I've never seen that anywhere else.

To be brief, since we couldn't reach you, Dad and Mom called your neighbor, Mrs. Fouillich. We thought her name was Fouillis and had a hard time finding her in the phone book. Finally, we got hold of her, and she told us that you were in the hospital because of your foot, which was swelling again.

So, Gran, if your foot keeps inflating, does that mean you're going to lift off soon?

Just kidding! I hope it's not serious. All the same, you could have told Dad, and Grandpa too, especially since he's your son—even if he is sixty years old! He wasn't aware that you were in the hospital either. Dad said we looked like dopes having to ask your neighbor about you.

What did you do with my kitten, which I know isn't completely mine, but almost mine, since Mom didn't say no? I don't think you can take a kitten with you to the hospital, not if it pees on the floor and scratches the curtains.

Mom says it must be with your neighbor,

Mrs. Fouillich. Let's hope so. I hope she's taking care of your cat too.

Please don't get the impression that I'm only thinking of the kitten and not about you. It's just that the kitten is so small and must be feeling lonely. At your age, you're more independent. . . . But I wouldn't like to be in your shoes. Hospitals scare me, so I won't be visiting you. I'd rather see you when your foot is deflated and you're back home with my little kitten.

> I kiss you tenderly,
> Annabelle

January 24

My dear granddaughter,

    How pleased I am to receive your letters! I don't read anything else. I asked Mrs. Fouillich to bring me all your mail from home so I could reread all that you've written. This is how I noticed that you never explained why you broke up with that friend of yours——the one with the pretty name, Lucia.

    In one letter, you allude to getting a zero in math, which I suspect might be the reason for your breakup. How can that be? One can't get angry over a poor test score! I don't understand. . . . Did something more serious happen that would explain why you don't like each other anymore? Because, you know, a broken friendship is as serious as a broken heart.

    I would like you to tell me what happened, because this

*makes me sad all of a sudden. Believe me, life is too short to
destroy a real love or a true friendship.*

    I kiss you tenderly.

Your Gran, who thinks of you a lot

*P.S. Your kitten is indeed with Mrs. Fouillich. The little
brat tears her TV guide every week, as soon as she takes it
out of its wrapping. So my poor friend has to watch the
stupidest things every night, now that she doesn't have the
program listings. But it doesn't matter much, since she falls
asleep after fifteen minutes in front of her TV anyway.*

P.P.S. Odd things seem to surprise you, my dear:

    *I don't have a dishwasher simply because I like to dip
my hands in water. And doing the dishes with a friend . . .
or a great-granddaughter . . . offers an ideal opportunity to
talk and unburden your heart. I remember that when my
little Annabelle was drying a plate in my kitchen, she told
me she was jealous of her brothers because they did many
things alone with their dad.*

As for my coffee grinder, it must be worth a fortune! It's very old. It belonged to my mother. I can still see her holding it between her knees while solemnly grinding coffee beans. She was always lost in thoughts that she kept to herself.

I look at this grinder now, I look at my hands, and it's as if I were continuing to grind very old coffee that my mother started and left me to finish.

I kiss you again, something I never tire of.

Gran

January 27

My darling little Gran,

I am so happy to hear from you at last. Do you know that I now use my ten fingers to type on the keyboard? It makes me feel like an adult—like a very efficient secretary. Dad is very proud of me.

I'm telling you this, my little Gran, because while typing my mail all these weeks, it occurred to me that maybe I could become a writer. What do you think? I spoke to Mom about it and she says it's very difficult to be a good writer. She'd rather I think about a job in data processing, since I enjoy playing on the computer.

See what I mean? There she goes again, doing the choosing for me. Well, enough about that.

I want to explain about Lucia. It seems funny,

since no one but you has asked what really happened between us. It's probably better that way; I'm not proud of what I did.

It happened the day we had a geometry test.

I couldn't draw my diagram.

I didn't understand a thing. I got tangled up in my medians and vertices. I was totally confused.

I whispered to Lucia to show me her paper so that I could copy the triangle she had made. She whispered back that she wasn't sure about what she'd done. I kept bugging her until she let me see her paper. And I copied everything. We handed in our tests. Of course, they were identical. I was hoping we'd done the problems right so that the teacher wouldn't notice anything strange.

But when we got our papers back, we both had a zero.

The teacher said:

"Since I've no way of knowing which one of you cheated, it's a zero for the two of you. If you find this unfair, the person who cheated can come and speak to me after class."

We both started to cry—Lucia because she had a zero she didn't deserve, and me because I was scared at the thought of what people would say if I confessed.

What's so weird is that the more Lucia cried, the angrier I got!

I told myself:

If she cries more than I do, then the others and the teacher will guess that I'm the one who cheated.

So I cried louder than Lucia.

At the end of class, the teacher asked very nicely:

"Come on, girls, be brave. Are you the one who cheated, Annabelle?"

Of course, I should have said "yes."

But the word "no" came out of my mouth instead.

Lucia had started sobbing again but stopped immediately. She looked at me hard, in a way that I can't even describe. Almost as if I were dog poop she'd just stepped in.

The teacher said:

"Too bad, girls! It's a matter between the two of you, then."

We left the room, and Lucia hasn't spoken to me since.

Now she sits next to Katia. As for me, sometimes I sit with Olivier, a nice boy who likes me. And sometimes I sit next to Fanny.

I don't want to have a best friend anymore . . . ever.

It's a good thing I'm not writing with a pen, because I'm crying as I tell you this. My tears would make the ink all blotchy, and you'd have little clouds of sadness all over the white sheet of paper.

Did I just write something poetic, Gran?

Anyway, I'm scared of what you're going to say. Please don't repeat what I just told you to a living soul, or else I'll never write to you again.

I swear it.

It's a secret, totally hush-hush between us, OK?

I sniffle as I send you kisses! (I know, it's pretty disgusting.)

Annabelle, the not so belle

January 30

Dear little one,

    My foot is hurting me a lot today, so I won't send you a long letter.

    It's incredible how pain can keep you from thinking.

    If I could cut off my foot, I'd do it!

    Yet in the past, I loved my feet.

    All this makes me think of your great-grandfather, my poor Lulu, who took me waltzing and tangoing. Oh, what marvelous tangos we danced when we were twenty years old! Lulu and I would go to ballroom after ballroom on Saturday nights. My feet were never tired back then. They glided and jumped. I was so light. Of course, you can't imagine that. You must think I was always the way I am now—a plump, crippled old lady—a heavy potato sack.

But I wasn't, dearest! I was light and graceful once. I never thought of my feet then.

It's never too soon to think about your own feet, Annabelle; they walk, they jump, they run, they are marvelous!

Suddenly I wonder who invented the expression "shoot yourself in the foot"!

I kiss you, my darling.

Your poor Gran, who thinks of you and of her feet with affection

February 3

My poor Gran,

I'm as mad as can be—all because of your last letter. You didn't even realize that I was anxiously waiting for your response. Now I wonder whether you got *my* letter? Or if you even read it?

Every day since I wrote to you, I've asked myself: "What did Gran think of what I told her about Lucia? Will she despise me now? Will she assume that I'm just an ugly little cheater?"

I even told myself that I would regret having written to you about what happened, that maybe you'd tell my parents; then I thought you were the only person I could have confessed to, because you have experience and give good advice. I guess I've been telling myself a lot of things.

My hands were shaking when I opened your letter! And what do you talk to me about? Your feet! I must be dreaming! Or as my brothers say when they think I'm acting crazy, I'm hallucinating!

Either way, I'm really at a loss.

Either you don't care about my problems, and this one in particular, or you're losing your mind.

In any case, you and I are no longer on the same wavelength.

56 So please excuse me, but I have schoolwork to do.

Annabelle

February 6

Dear Annabelle,

I thought the silly age was more or less around four-teen. Yet, if I remember properly, you're only eleven years old. At least in this respect, you're precocious for your age.

I don't write as often now. I just don't have the courage to answer you. I'm not really mad at you. I'm simply tired.

Talk to you later.

Kisses,
Gran

P.S. I hear that your father may be coming to visit me. Tell him to fetch your kitten at Mrs. Fouillich's before she gives it to an animal shelter.

February 11

Dear Gran,

I don't remember what I wrote to you last time, but obviously you weren't pleased.

What I recall is that your answer was totally beside the point, which made me angry. But, as you already told me once, if I don't like what you have to say, I can write to Cousin Amélie instead.

I wish you wouldn't be upset with me, though, because I've gotten used to receiving your letters. They're like an addiction! If I don't get any letters from you in the future, I'll miss them terribly.

Dad is definitely going to visit you at the hospital this weekend. Without Mom. She thinks driving four hundred kilometers there and back is a lot of road time. Don't be upset. It's not that she doesn't like you enough to make the trip, just that she has so much to do here on Saturdays and Sundays. Like catching up with the laundry, housecleaning, and errands to run. (It's my birthday next month and I think she's going to buy my present this weekend. I asked for a Discman.)

Dad will visit you on his own, and he'll bring back the kitten!

Since you probably won't be able to send me something for my birthday, I'm going to consider the kitten my Christmas and birthday present rolled in one. A heartfelt thanks!

I hope your foot is better and that you can start thinking about something else soon. I can't imagine how boring it must be to dwell on nothing but one's feet all day long.

Your little Annabelle, who loves you

P.S. I'm not eleven but twelve years old. Don't try to shrink me! I'm already small for my age. Small at all levels, in fact, physically and morally (reread my letter where I tell you about my stupid blunders, so stupid that you probably thought they didn't deserve an answer).

P.P.S. I forgot to tell you that a friend of mine is having a fancy Mardi Gras costume party at her house. I'm not going. I'm too old for a costume. Besides, I wouldn't know what to wear.

Jonathan said:

"Go as a monster, so you won't have to dress up."

That made me cry.

Jules made fun of me too when he added:

"Or go as a mourner from ancient times. You won't have much to do either!"

Mom said this was somewhat true. She thinks I've been whimpering a lot lately.

"This party will do you good," she told me. "We'll find the right costume, you'll see."

Which means I have to come up with an idea

before she does—or else she's going to be deciding for me again.

S.O.S. Gran, do you have a suggestion? Please hurry—the party is thirteen days away.

February 18

Dear Gran,

Dad is back with the kitten!

I can't tell you how adorable he is!

He scratches me a little because he's not used to me yet. But he sleeps at the foot of my bed, which makes me feel peaceful as I fall asleep.

Jules and Jonathan are jealous. But Dad told them the kitten was mine and that I was the one who would care for him. I went to buy a litter box, and cans of cat food and everything. Next week I'm taking him to the vet for his shots.

Having a kitten must be like taking care of a baby. So I'm very careful. Mom says it's good to be responsible for something, that it's part of the process of growing up. Of course, sometimes it can be annoying to have such a responsibility. For instance, last night I was watching a cool movie on TV when the kitten started meowing. I didn't go see what was happening right away, and suddenly Mom shouted:

"Annabelle, your kitten did not use his litter box. The bathroom door was closed! Now you'll have to clean up the mess."

I told Mom I'd do it after the movie, but she said no.

"You'll take care of it right away, please; it stinks in the hallway."

And true enough, it did stink.

Jules and Jonathan were laughing as they held their noses. I gave the kitten a gentle slap, but it didn't bother him much. He just ran off to play with the curtain!

Mom shouted again while I still had my hands in the kitten's mess:

"Annabelle, get your kitten away from the curtain or else all your money will be spent on buying a new one!"

I sure didn't want *that,* because once I get the Discman for my birthday, I intend to buy as much music as I can.

So thanks to my misbehaving kitten, I missed half of the movie. But it doesn't matter, since I'm very happy to have him. When I come home in the afternoon, he looks at me and stretches on my bed to be stroked. I whisper sweet things to him until he purrs.

I think he loves me.

And because Lucia doesn't love me anymore, it makes me happy.

Get better soon, Gran. I'll visit you at Easter, as always.

Lots of kisses,
Annabelle

P.S. Thank you again for Zip. That's what I just named the kitten.

65

February 20

Dear Gran,

What is this thing, Gran? This funny-looking package filled with old clothes that the post office delivered this morning and that was sent overnight by Mrs. Fouillich???

Mom says the clothes are ancient but very chic. Were they yours? It's a mystery. No letter came with them. What are they for? Are you giving them to me so that I'll remember you when you're dead?

Please, answer me.

Big kisses,
Annabelle

P.S. Dad just came home. We showed him the old stuff you sent me. He stood scratching his forehead, then said:

"Shoot! Gran told me about the package in the hospital, but I forgot. She asked Mrs. Fouillich to look for old clothes in Gran's attic and send them to Annabelle so that she can dress up for her party."

I don't know what I'll look like in these clothes, but at least I'll be unique. Thanks for thinking of me, Gran. I'll keep you posted.

February 26

Dear Gran,

I worry about you.

I overheard Dad talking with Grandpa on the phone. He said your foot was so bad it might be necessary to amputate it.

Cut off your foot!

I didn't even know it was possible to do that.

I don't want this to happen to you! It sounds horrible.

I understand now why you were talking about your foot in your last letter.

In my opinion, they won't amputate it. It'll get better.

After all, if it's possible to implant a pig's heart in

humans with bad hearts, I can't believe that a swollen foot can't be cured.

Now I think of hardly anything else but your foot. It's catching, I guess!

But I'll make an effort.

You know, sending me your old clothes was a super idea. It gave me a weird feeling to slip into your dresses at first, almost as if I were disguising myself as you. A younger you, of course. I'm already taller than you were, my little Gran. You're really a tiny one! Mom added a flounce at the bottom of the blue dress. She put my hair up in a bun and pinned your small hat on. I lent her my camera and she took a picture of me, which I'm sending to you now. I hope you'll like it.

Do you think I look like you?

Lucia, the friend I told you about, was at the party disguised as Charlie Chaplin's Tramp. That's from a movie from your younger days, isn't it? Lucia looked at me and I looked at her. But we didn't talk.

I had fun, anyway! Being dressed in your clothes made me feel as if you were there too.

I danced a lot.

Which reminds me of your foot again. They're not going to cut it off, are they? Or is it really going to happen?

I kiss you a thousand times.

Your great-granddaughter,
who thinks of you often,
Annabelle

March 1

My dearest grandchild,

    On the eve of my surgery, I write you this letter. That goes to show you how important it is.

    You see, while one day it may be possible to implant a pig's heart in a human, my foot cannot be saved. That's the way it is. Anyway, I wouldn't look too good with a pig's foot instead of my own.

    But this is not the reason I am writing to you.

    I am going to talk about Lucia.

    You're probably thinking:

    "When I expect to hear about Lucia, Gran talks about her foot; and when I expect to hear about her foot, Gran talks about Lucia." Old people are very baffling, I suppose.

    Tonight, in fact, I don't want to think about my foot.

I already took it off the list of invited guests for the evening——even the rest of my life.

I want to spend this evening in your company, in Lucia's and also in Zelia's. The very moment you mentioned Lucia to me, Zelia came back to me in a flash. Maybe it's the similarity between the two names.

You see, I also had a very dear friend. And I lost her. Forever.

We had been friends from early childhood. We went to the same school, we did our hair the same way (our mothers used metallic rollers that we slept in all night long, and in the morning, they would gather our curls back with a nice ribbon). I adored Zelia.

She was pretty, my God how pretty she was, much prettier than me. When we were children, this wasn't a problem; neither one of us thought about it.

I helped Zelia with her homework. I kept her apprised of my catechism lessons, because she didn't attend the class and I feared that death would separate us forever; she would be in hell with the unbelievers, and I would be in heaven, lonely without her.

I attended school longer than she did; her parents thought it was sufficient for a girl to read and write.

So Zelia and I found ourselves separated.

Whenever I saw her, I tried to pass on all that I had learned at school. But it bothered her. Now that she was no longer attending classes, academic lessons were far from her mind.

She wanted to talk only of her love life.

And I was constantly lecturing her, like a paragon of morality.

She got fed up. One day, she shouted in my face:

"Keep this up and nobody will ever love you!"

She probably touched a sore point. Especially since I always trusted what she said. So I had no reason not to believe her then.

Her comment made me hate her intensely and with all my heart. I could see in her eyes that she hated me too.

It was as if she had jinxed me.

As if what she'd said would come true.

I kept telling myself:

"Now nobody will ever love me. It's over."

I thought I had forgotten all these memories. Because, of course, I found love. Otherwise you wouldn't be here, my darling granddaughter.

Over the years, I often thought of Zelia. I wondered what had happened to her, if she had been happy. I'd love to think she was. Now I wonder whether she's dead, and if she's in heaven waiting for me. Whether she remembers me at all.

So you see, on the eve of the painful days to come, I still think of her as I write to you . . . just as much as I think of you.

I miss Zelia.

Are you too young to understand?

I don't think so.

The night nurse just passed by and asked if I was writing my will.

"It looks like a long one," she said. "You must have a lot to leave behind." Then she smiled and added softly, "Don't you worry. Everything will be fine."

I don't worry too much. Just enough, I believe. And I don't have much to leave.

The most important is this piece of advice: Don't wait till tomorrow to give the love you can provide today.

I have your picture on my bedside table. I'm not sure whether you look like me or not. I like to think you don't resemble anyone, and that's fine.

I kiss you even more tenderly than usual.

Don't forget me.

Your Gran, who loves you much

March 4

Dear Gran,

Your letter brought tears to my eyes.

I know that the surgery was a success but that you're in a lot of pain.

I don't know what to say, and yet I feel that I want to tell you so many things. It's all a muddle in my head: your foot, the pain, my fear, Zelia, Lucia, you and me.

I've never suffered much that I can recall, and I'm a bit ashamed of the fuss I made when my four wisdom teeth had to be pulled. Certainly nothing compared to your foot being amputated.

I thought I was in pain then. . . . Now I'm not so sure.

What can I say that could cheer you up?

Spring is coming. The weather is very mild. Zip, the kitten you gave me, is crazy happy. He goes out of the house, but the garden seems too small for him. He wants more space, and we have a hard time making him come home. I feel like jumping, running, and wandering around too. When I realize what's happening to you, I remember what you told me once: Take advantage of your feet while you have them.

And I will—until I drop.

I'm even beginning to like the ballet class that I hated months ago. Now I feel more comfortable on my toes, lighter too.

Don't you think spring makes you feel that way?

You know, Gran, more and more I think about becoming a writer. And it's thanks to you. I began to enjoy writing when I started sending you letters. I'll dedicate my first book to you.

So hang on. Stay alive until then.

A thousand kisses.

See you soon. (At Easter like always.)

Annabelle

March 6

Dear Gran,

I know you feel a bit better thanks to Grandpa, who called to give us the latest update.

We're having the usual March hailstorms. It irritates Mom. When she goes out with her umbrella, it doesn't rain or hail and she carries it for nothing; when she doesn't take the umbrella, it rains cats and dogs and she comes back drenched. It makes me laugh, because she hates it. I don't know why, but I love the rain these days. It's a new feeling. It's like it washes my hair, like it cleanses me completely.

I'm going to talk about myself in this letter.

Not everything is fine. Dad and Mom saw my report card and got angry.

I won't get the Discman for my birthday. Mom

already bought it, but she's putting it aside until my schoolwork improves.

No birthday party either! It's lucky the invitations weren't sent out yet. Otherwise I'd be humiliated.

Fortunately, there is Olivier. I've mentioned him before. He's a nice boy, crazy about movies. He writes little scenarios, and his buddy, Pierrick, makes comic strips out of them. Then they pass them on to me to read. They tell me not to spare their feelings, to be as critical as I want, like a real newspaper reviewer. But as soon as I say: "I don't like this part too much . . ." they attack me like tigers defending their cubs.

Still, I'm glad I made these new friends. If Lucia hadn't gotten mad at me, I would never have grown close to either Olivier or Pierrick, and our friendship has taught me a lot, probably because they're both very different from me.

I realize that when I was with Lucia, like you with Zelia, we always wanted to do and see the same things, wear similar clothes, etc. Now I'm conscious that I can be friends with people who aren't like me, and who I don't want to look like either.

Of course, I never told Olivier or Pierrick that I'm a cheater and a liar. But I'm discovering that you don't have to tell your friends everything. Olivier and Pierrick don't talk about themselves. We talk about movies, music, and TV shows. We don't necessarily like or watch the same stuff, which is just as well too.

That's it.

So I'm happy not to be alone anymore. But I still miss Lucia.

There are things I feel I could tell to her only, but I miss her for other reasons.

I can't explain these reasons. The words don't come easily.

I'm sure you understand, don't you, my little Gran?

I hope with all my heart that your pain eases.

I'm impatiently waiting to see you at Easter.

Although we didn't celebrate my thirteenth birthday the way I had hoped, I've grown a lot lately. Do you notice the difference in my letters?

I kiss you very tenderly, darling Gran.
Annabelle

March 9

My dear Annabelle,

I haven't the courage to write a long letter, but I want to tell you that I believe I understand what you're saying about your feelings for Lucia.

(As you can see, I'm improving. For once, I don't mention my foot when you talk about your friend.)

There is a beautiful phrase someone wrote, though I no longer remember who (pardon this slip of memory), about a dear friend of his: "If you urge me to explain why I liked him, it can't be expressed other than by saying: because it was him, because it was me."

You see, there I go again playing teacher. I probably can't help it!

There is nothing else to say: I loved Zelia because she was Zelia and you love Lucia because she is Lucia.

So tell yourself that Lucia probably also loves you as you are. Even if you are a bit of a cheater, a bit of a liar. Cheer up, my darling.

Your Gran, who thinks of you

P.S. It bothered me not to remember the name of the writer, so I asked Mrs. Fouillich, who immediately said, "It's Montaigne!" That could be true. But you should check, because my neighbor's memory is not as good as she thinks it is, and I wouldn't want you to learn the wrong thing.

March 12

Dear dear dear Gran,

Your letters make me cry sometimes.

You were right to play teacher! What a beautiful thought you sent me about friendship! I'll remember it all my life!

You really believe that I could be loved as I am?

I find myself so *ugly* sometimes. From all points of view.

I'm not at all as I would like to be.

But what is there to do? Do you believe we have more than one chance at life? That we can be reincarnated?

Until next time,
Annabelle

March 15

My faithful Annabelle,

> *One has a thousand opportunities in life.*
> *Even perhaps a million opportunities.*
> *In fact, one has a chance every day, every hour, even*
> *every minute.*
> *So go ahead, seize them.*
> *I kiss you with all my heart,*

Gran

91

March 17

Dear Annabelle,

Your father phoned and told me that your kitten is a she!!! Is this an early April Fools' joke?

I find it terribly amusing.

So he is a Zipette!!

The cat, not your father, of course!

I have to go now. They are taking me to rehab.

Huge smooches (see, I'm in the know!),

Gran

March 20

Dearest Gran,

Dad and Mom came back very saddened from visiting you.

They say you're taking very strong sedatives to alleviate the pain from your amputation. I wonder how it's possible to still feel your foot when it's no longer there.

Maybe it's similar to the pain from a severed friendship. Like your friendship with Zelia. It was a long time ago and yet you're still suffering. What do you think?

I'm trying to change my life.

I spoke to Lucia last Tuesday. I took my chances. I sat next to her. We didn't speak at all for the first hour of class. Then we exchanged little notes. I find it easier to say serious things in writing now, maybe because I've gotten used to writing to you.

I was shaking when I passed along my first note. It said:

"Can you be my friend again?"

I didn't write "my best friend," because I thought it would be asking too much.

She didn't answer. She seemed troubled.

So I sent her another note.

"I apologize for the zero in math."

She answered right away:

"That's not important anymore."

"What's the matter, then?" I wrote back.

It took her a long time to answer. I could see that she was writing, erasing, writing. Finally she crumpled the note, which got me upset.

I grabbed the ball of crumpled paper in spite of Lucia's protests and read it.

She had written a lot of things, but I remember this particularly:

"I don't know if we can be friends again because I don't like you as I did in the past."

It hurt me a lot to read Lucia's feelings, but what she wrote is true. I know that I can live without her too.

I also know that I wouldn't be as happy.

That's what I told her during class break.

"It makes me sad not to be friendly with you anymore."

"Me too," she said.

You see, Gran, we talked and the sadness didn't go away. We still have this weight on our chests. We're no longer the same people, I suppose.

This is a long letter. I hope reading it won't tire you.

I kiss you tenderly,
Annabelle

*(I don't know what day it is and
I really don't care.)*

Dear Gran,

    *I'm very concerned about you. Grandpa called
to say that you have a problem with your heart
and that, at your age, the doctors fear the worst.*

    *No, not you, I beg you! I'm not using the com-
puter to write to you this time, because in your first
letter—which I just read again—you said how
much you had loved my old handwritten letters,
spelling mistakes and all.*

    *So I think that with a pen I'll express different
words—real words that come straight from my
heart.*

    *I can make new friends, but I could never have
a Gran other than you.*

Please, dear Gran, don't die.

I think of you so often that you can't possibly die.

I love you with all my heart,
Annabelle

March 30

My little Gran,

How wonderful to hear that you're better! The doctor says you're surprisingly strong. I knew it! Very often I'm told that I look like you. Well, that makes me extra happy if it also means that I have your strength.

I have only good news for you.

First, Lucia and I are friends again, but not like before. We're not glued to each other. When we spend time together we talk about everything and nothing. When we're apart it's not tragic. I discuss movies with Pierrick and Olivier (more about him and my suspicions that he may have a crush on me in my next letter; Lucia says it's just wishful thinking on my part, but I don't think so).

Lucia is still friends with Katia. Sometimes the three of us hang out, which isn't bad. Katia is outrageously funny. When she bursts out laughing, you can't help laughing too. Actually, the three of us have gotten punished several times because of it.

We don't care.

It's important to have a good laugh! We only have one life, don't we, Gran?

The last piece of good news is that Zip had kittens. There's an almost entirely white one that Olivier's mother will take after Easter break. A tiger-like one that Katia is begging her mother to adopt (and I don't see who could resist Katia). And a little black one that nobody wants for the time being, although he's adorable. Dad and Mom say it's because lots of people are superstitious and believe that black cats bring bad luck.

My darling little Gran, I leave you now. See you soon. Easter is around the corner.

> Your great-granddaughter,
> who loves you so much,
> Annabelle

Palm Sunday

My dearest granddaughter,

You're right, Easter is nearly here, and I feel resurrected!

Yet not so long ago, I had no desire to live.

It seemed that no solid thread was linking me to Earth. But as you see, one cannot know what life holds or what death is.

It's tempting to say that life is the opposite of death . . . but I believe this is false.

When I felt at death's door, it was as if my body had become a burden that kept me from living in the moment and from being free. I was tired of that body, but not of life! Not of life, Annabelle.

I wanted to tell you that, for next time . . . for when I really die.

You'll be able to listen to the organ and say to yourself: Death is not the opposite of life. It's just the other side, perhaps—the flip side.

I love you dearly, and I'll be happy to share some more beautiful days with you. Hopping along, of course.

A poet by the name of Blaise Cendrars, who lost an arm during the First World War (yes, always this awful war), thought that his hand had become a constellation in the sky. So if you notice a constellation in the shape of a foot, don't forget to mention it to me. It would be consoling to see my foot winking at me from above!

The sky is beautiful today and Earth even more so!

I kiss you, my darling. See you soon.

Gran

P.S. By the way, when you come next Sunday, please bring me the black kitten that supposedly brings bad luck. I have nothing more to fear!

Notes

Abd al-Rahmān I (731–788): Born in Damascus, Syria, Abd al-Rahmān was the son of an Umayyad prince. In 750, he was one of a few members of his family to escape slaughter at the hands of a rival clan. Al-Rahmān made his way to Córdoba, the capital of Islamic Spain, where he ruled for thirty-two years.

Blaise Cendrars (1887–1961): Pseudonym of Frédéric Sauser. Born in Switzerland, Cendrars moved to Paris in 1910, where he established himself as a poet and novelist. Two of his most famous books, *I Have Killed* and *The Severed Hand,* were based on his experience as a soldier in the First World War. Cendrars served from December 1914 until September 1915. He lost his right arm in battle in September 1915.

Chemin des Dames (Ladies' Path): Located northeast of Paris, between the towns of Soissons and Laon, the Chemin des Dames runs west to east for some thirty kilometers along a ridge that separates the rivers Aisne and Ailette. It got its name back in the eighteenth century, when the two daughters of Louis XV, Adélaïde and Victoire, traveled the path to get from Paris to the Château de La Bove near Vauclair.

Of strategic importance and the site of three major battles during the First World War, the Chemin des Dames witnessed the fiercest combat between April 16 and April 25, 1917. French forces were unable to push back German forces and lost about 187,000 men.

First World War (1914–1918): Also known as the Great War, World War I, and the War to End All Wars, this military conflict took place mostly in Europe. It was a war waged between the Allied Powers: mainly France, Great Britain, Russia, Italy (from 1915 on), Japan, and the United States (from 1917 on), against the Central Powers: Austria–Hungary, Germany, Bulgaria, and the Ottoman Empire. The Allies prevailed—but not before at least eight million soldiers and nine million civilians died (estimates vary and can be higher).

Louis XVI (1754–1793): Louis XVI ruled as King of France from 1774 to 1792. His wife was Marie Antoinette. Under their reign, the spread of poverty and social unrest caused the population of France to rebel, giving rise to the French Revolution. Both Louis XVI and Marie Antoinette were taken prisoner, along with countless others, and sentenced to death by the guillotine.

Michel de Montaigne (1533–1592): Montaigne was one of the most influential writers of the French Renaissance and is heralded for having popularized the essay form. His massive five-volume *Essais* (*Essays*) contains some of the most influential essays ever written. He did indeed write: "Because it was him, because it was me," which can be found in Volume I.

Umayyads: The Umayyad dynasty ruled in Damascus, Syria, from 661 to 750. They were overthrown by a rival clan, the Abbāsids.

About the Author

Jo Hoestlandt has written many novels for young readers in her native France. She has always enjoyed telling stories, which she likens to being a magician. For a long time, she has participated in children's reading and writing workshops. She lives in a suburb of Paris and has three grown children.

About the Illustrator

Born in Lorient (French Brittany), Aurélie Abolivier studied art in Brest, graphic design in Paris, and illustration in Strasbourg. She now lives in Paris and illustrates children's books.

Just like Annabelle, Aurélie Abolivier waits impatiently for the mail—especially from her aunt, who sends her handmade postcards, intricately designed envelopes, and, once, painted oysters with Abolivier's address tucked inside (thank you, mail carrier!).